OXFORD BOOKWORMS LIBRARY
Classics

Animal Farm

GEORGE ORWELL

Level 3 (1000 headwords)

Retold by Nicole Irving
Illustrated by János Orban

Series Editor: Rachel Bladon
Editor: Madeleine Burgess

OXFORD
UNIVERSITY PRESS

Great Clarendon Street, Oxford, OX2 6DP, United Kingdom

Oxford University Press is a department of the University of Oxford.
It furthers the University's objective of excellence in research, scholarship,
and education by publishing worldwide. Oxford is a registered trade
mark of Oxford University Press in the UK and in certain other countries

ISBN: 978 0 19 426753 3   Book
ISBN: 978 0 19 426750 2   Book and audio pack

For more information on the Oxford Bookworms Library,
visit www.oup.com/elt/gradedreaders

ACKNOWLEDGEMENTS

Cover images by: Shutterstock (foxaon1987, Hein Nouwens,
Ilias Bekyashev, Naniti, Rustic, Studio Ayutaka)

Illustrations by: János Orban

*The publisher would like to thank the following for their permission to reproduce
photographs*: Alamy Stock Photo (Juniors Bildarchiv GmbH, Masterpics);
Getty Images (brandstaetter images); Shutterstock (AnetaPics, Geza Farkas,
Glasshouse Images, Hintau Aliaksei, kvasilev, Nataly Studio)

This adaptation of *Animal Farm* is dedicated to the memory of my friend and
colleague, Rachel Bladon.   Nicole Irving

The manufacturer's authorised representative in the EU for product safety
is Oxford University Press España S.A. of El Parque Empresarial San
Fernando de Henares, Avenida de Castilla, 2 – 28830 Madrid
(www.oup.es/en or product.safety@oup.com). OUP España S.A. also acts
as importer into Spain of products made by the manufacturer.

CONTENTS

ANIMALS IN THIS STORY

Old Major
Snowball
Napoleon
Squealer
} pigs

Boxer
Clover
Mollie
} horses

Benjamin   a donkey
Muriel   a goat

PEOPLE IN THIS STORY

Mr Jones   the farmer who owns Manor Farm
Mrs Jones   Mr Jones's wife
Mr Whymper   the business person who helps Napoleon

CHAPTER 1

Major's Dream

Mr Jones of Manor Farm had locked the chicken houses for the night, although he had missed a few. He walked towards the farmhouse in a straightish line and pulled his boots off as he went into the kitchen. Then he got himself one last beer and went upstairs to bed, where Mrs Jones was already asleep.

Mr Jones pulled his boots off as he went into the kitchen.

When the bedroom light went off, all the animals in the farm buildings began to move quietly. They had heard that Major, the oldest pig on the farm, had had a strange dream and wanted to talk about it with the animals. So, they had decided to meet in the big barn after Mr Jones was in bed. Old Major was an important and special animal for all the other animals on the farm – he had lived a long life and understood things, so they were happy to lose an hour's sleep to listen to him.

When the animals began to arrive in the barn, Old Major was already there, resting comfortably at one end of the building. He was twelve years old and had recently grown large, but he was still a good-looking pig, with a kind, intelligent face. The three farm dogs came in first, and then the pigs, who sat down in front of Old Major. Some of the chickens and other farm birds followed, and then the sheep and the cows walked in and lay down behind the pigs.

Next, the two large farm horses, Boxer and Clover, slowly came in together. They stepped carefully because they did not want to hurt any small animal that was perhaps hidden underneath their feet. Clover was a big, strong, motherly horse who had had four babies. Boxer was the largest animal on the farm and as strong as two horses. He was not the most intelligent animal, but all the others liked him because he was calm and sensible, and he never stopped working.

After the two horses, Muriel the white goat and Benjamin the donkey arrived. Benjamin was older than all the other animals, and he was often cross. He never said much, and he was the only one of the farm animals who never laughed. If you asked him why, he said that he saw nothing to laugh about. He loved Boxer with all his heart, although he never said so.

The two horses had just sat down when more farm birds arrived, and Clover made a safe place for them between her big feet. Lastly, Mollie the pretty, young white horse came in and looked around as she danced her way to the front. She wanted everyone to notice her. The farm cat appeared, too, and soon found a warm bed between Clover and Boxer and fell asleep.

Old Major waited patiently until all the animals were comfortable, and then he began to speak.

'Comrades,' he said, 'before I tell you about the strange dream that I had last night, there's another thing that I would like to say. I have lived a long time and thought a lot about the life we animals have in this world. Before I die, I must explain to you a few of the things that I have learned.

'Now, comrades, think about it: our lives are miserable. They are hard and short, and filled with work. We are given just enough food and no more, and every working animal spends long hours in the fields. No farm animal in England knows what happiness is. No farm animal is free.

'Is this natural? Is it because our country is poor? Is it because this farm is poor? No, comrades. No, no, no. This farm can easily make enough food for us all to eat and live well. So, why do our lives continue in this miserable way? Because of humans! They take everything that we make; they steal it.

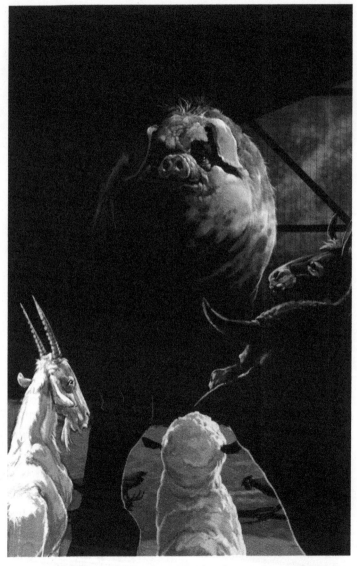

'*Humans take everything that we make; they steal it,*' said Major.

'Cows, people take your milk and sell it for money; chickens, they take your eggs. And you, Clover, where are the four babies that you loved? Each of those young horses was sold when it was a year old, and you will never see them again. What did the humans give you for them, Clover, and for all your years of work in the fields? Nothing, except a little food and a place for sleeping in a barn.

'Our miserable lives are made very short because we are sold as meat. You pigs, for example, most of you will be dead in a year. Is it not clear then, comrades, that we need to fight against the humans who make our lives so difficult? We must work night and day to chase them off the land. Then, we animals can begin to work together, for ourselves, and we can be happy and free. That is my message to you, comrades: Rebellion!

'I don't know when that Rebellion will come – perhaps in a week, perhaps in a hundred years, but a time will come when animals will stand up against humans, I am sure of that. You must give my message to your children and ask them to give it to their children, too. And always, you must work together as comrades and friends to fight against people. All humans are enemies. All animals are comrades. Anything that walks on two legs is an enemy. Anything that walks on four legs or has wings is a friend.

'Remember, as you fight against humans, don't become like them. No animal must ever live in a house, sleep in a bed, wear clothes, drink beer, or buy and sell things with money. No animal must ever use a whip against another animal, or be violent towards one. Animals must all live and work together, like brothers and sisters. Clever or stupid, big or small, we're all comrades. No animal must ever kill any other animal. All animals are equal.

'And now, I will tell you about my dream,' continued Old Major. 'I dreamt about a wonderful world without people, and this made me remember something. Many years ago, when I was a little pig, my mother and her friends used to sing an old song to me. I'd forgotten it, but last night it came back to me in my dream. I remember it so clearly now. I am old and my voice is not strong, but I will sing it to you, and after I have taught you, you can sing it better for yourselves. Its name is *Animals of the world*.

It was true, Old Major's voice was not strong, but he sang well enough:

Animals of this land,
Animals of the world,
Farm animals everywhere,
Listen to my wonderful news
Of the golden future time.

The day is coming soon,
When animals can work the land
Without people and their whips,
When animals are free
And everything that they make is theirs.

Animals of this land,
Animals of the world,
Farm animals everywhere,
Come together to make this happen,
This golden future time.

The animals had listened to Old Major with growing excitement and were beginning to sing the song themselves before he had even finished. The cleverest ones, like the pigs and the dogs, remembered all the words immediately and started to sing it again. Soon all the other animals had joined them, and together they sang *Animals of the world* five times.

But the noise from the barn woke up Mr Jones, who thought that there must be a wild animal on the farm. He jumped out of bed, picked up his gun, and shot it into the night from the bedroom window. In the barn, everyone hurried away towards their sleeping places, and soon, the farm was asleep.

Chapter 2

The Rebellion

Three nights later, Old Major died peacefully in his sleep. It was early March, and during the next three months, there was much secret work among the farm animals. Old Major's talk had changed how the more intelligent animals looked at life. They knew that the Rebellion may perhaps not happen in their lifetime, but that they must work to get things ready for when it came.

Two young pigs called Snowball and Napoleon did all the planning. This seemed natural because everyone knew that the pigs were the cleverest animals on the farm. Napoleon was a large animal who never said much, but usually got what he wanted. Snowball was quick and clever with words and always had lots of ideas. Another young pig, who worked closely with these two, was a small, fat one with a very round face and bright eyes called Squealer. When he spoke, everyone listened to him. He moved from side to side and waved his tail quickly when he was explaining anything difficult, and, for some reason, this made everyone believe what he was saying. 'He can change black into white,' the animals all said.

These three pigs had worked hard to bring together Old Major's ideas into a new way of thinking, which they called Animalism. Several nights each week, after Mr Jones and his wife were asleep in bed, the pigs had secret meetings in the barn and taught the other animals about the ideas of Animalism.

The three pigs worked hard to bring together Old Major's ideas.

At first, the animals did not listen carefully; some were not interested in what the pigs were saying. 'We should follow Mr Jones's orders. We're his animals,' some said, or, 'Mr Jones gives us food. We'll die without him.' Others asked questions like, 'Why must we care about what happens after we're dead?' or, 'Old Major said the Rebellion's going to happen. So why do we need to do anything?'

Mollie the pretty, white horse asked the stupidest questions. Her first was, 'Will there still be sugar after the Rebellion?'

'No,' Snowball said. 'We can't make sugar here. Also, you don't need sugar.'

'Will I still be able to wear ribbons in my hair?' Mollie then asked.

'Comrade,' said Snowball, 'when people see those ribbons, they know that you belong to humans. It's more important to be free than to wear ribbons, don't you understand?'

Mollie agreed, but did not seem very sure.

The animals who listened most carefully at the pigs' secret meetings were the two farm horses, Boxer and Clover. They were not clever, but after they had accepted the pigs as their teachers, they listened carefully to everything that they were told. Then they explained Animalism to the other animals on the farm with words that everyone could understand. The horses came to every secret meeting and always started the singing of *Animals of the world*, which ended each meeting.

The Rebellion happened much sooner and more easily than any of the animals had hoped. In the past, Mr Jones had managed his farm well, and it had been successful. But in recent times, he had lost a lot of money and begun drinking too much beer. He spent his days indoors, reading newspapers and drinking, and his farm workers were lazy, so now nobody was taking good care of the fields or farm buildings, and the animals did not get enough food.

One day in June, when the hay was almost ready for cutting, Mr Jones went into Willingdon, the nearby village, where he drank beer all evening. He did not come home until the next morning, and because he felt very ill, he went to bed and slept all day. The workers had milked the cows early that morning, but no one had given the animals their food, and when evening came, the animals were still hungry. They waited and waited, but at last, they could not wait any more. One of the cows broke the door to the shed where their food was kept, and all the animals came to get some.

Just then, Mr Jones woke up, and he and four of his workers quickly came outside. They beat the animals wildly with their whips, trying to chase them away from the shed. But this was too much for the hungry animals, and they immediately threw themselves at Jones and his workers and fought back in every possible way. Nothing like this had happened on the farm before, and the men could not stop the angry animals.

'Run!' shouted Jones at last. 'Or the animals will kill us!'

They ran down the small road that went to the entrance of the farm, and the animals chased them through the gate and closed it behind them.

Mrs Jones looked out of the bedroom window, saw what was happening, packed a small bag, and quickly left the farm by a different way. And so, the Rebellion had happened, and the animals had been successful: Jones had gone, and Manor Farm was theirs.

CHAPTER 3

The Seven Commandments

For the first few minutes, the animals could not believe their luck. They ran around the farm and checked to make sure that there really were no humans hiding anywhere. Then they hurried back to the farm buildings to destroy anything that Jones and his workers had used against them.

They found a cupboard full of whips and threw them all on a fire, and Snowball also burned the ribbons that the horses wore on market days. 'Ribbons,' he said, 'are clothes really, and clothes are for humans only; animals shouldn't wear clothes.' When Boxer heard this, he fetched the small hat that he had loved to wear in the summer to keep the flies off his ears, and he threw it on the fire, too.

In a short time, the animals had destroyed everything that reminded them of Mr Jones. Napoleon took them all back to the barn and gave them some extra food. Then they sang *Animals of the world* seven times, and after that they went to bed and slept better than they had ever slept before.

The next day, they woke early, and when they remembered the wonderful thing that had happened the day before, they all ran out into the fields together. They went up the little hill that was the highest place on the farm, and from the top, they stared down at everything: the fields, the fruit trees, the old walls around the outside of the farm. It was hard to believe, but all of it was now their own, and for a while, they jumped and danced happily and ate the sweet grass from the ground.

It was hard to believe, but all of it was now their own.

When they walked back to the farm buildings, they stopped in silence outside the farmhouse. That was theirs, too, but they were frightened to go inside at first. Then, after a moment, Snowball and Napoleon pushed the door open with their shoulders and everyone went in, stepping carefully behind each other in a line. They went slowly from room to room, speaking only in whispers as they stared at the comfortable chairs, the nice carpets, and the warm beds.

When they were leaving, they found Mollie in the best bedroom. She had taken a blue ribbon from Mrs Jones's table and was looking at herself in the mirror. 'What are you doing, Mollie?' the others said. 'Animals shouldn't wear ribbons.'

Outside, they talked together about the farmhouse. 'An animal must never live there,' they agreed. 'We must keep it as a special place to remind ourselves how humans lived and how terrible their ways were.'

'Before we start work today, comrades,' said Snowball, 'there's something that we must do.' The pigs told the others that, in the past three months, they had learned to read and write from old books. Then they all went to the farm gate, and Snowball (who was best at writing) painted over the old farm name and wrote 'ANIMAL FARM' in big letters.

The animals walked back to the farm buildings, to the end wall of the barn, and the pigs explained that they had brought together all the important messages and ideas of Animalism into Seven Commandments. 'You must learn these Seven Commandments, and you must always do what they say,' they told the animals. Snowball then climbed up beside the black barn wall (and it is not easy for a pig to climb). Then he and began writing in big, white letters:

THE SEVEN COMMANDMENTS
1 Anything that walks on two legs is an enemy.
2 Anything that walks on four legs or has wings is a friend.
3 Animals must not wear clothes.
4 Animals must not sleep in beds.
5 Animals must not drink beer or whisky.
6 No animal must ever kill any other animal.
7 All animals are equal.

These were nicely painted, except 'friend' was written 'freind'. Snowball read the Commandments aloud, and the animals all agreed with them. The cleverest ones began learning them at once.

'Now, comrades,' said Snowball, throwing down the paintbrush. 'Let's go to the fields and cut the hay. And let's do it faster than Jones and his workers ever did!'

But at that moment the cows, who had seemed very uncomfortable for a while, started to make loud noises because no one had milked them yet. The pigs soon found a way to do this and quickly filled five large bottles with lovely milk, which a few of the other animals looked at with great interest.

'Snowball began writing in big, white letters.'

'What will happen to that milk?' someone asked.

'Don't worry about the milk,' cried Napoleon. 'It's more important to cut the hay. Comrade Snowball will take you to the field that we're cutting today. I'll follow in a few minutes. Go, comrades!'

So the animals walked down to the fields to cut the hay, and when they came back in the evening, the milk had disappeared.

CHAPTER 4

Happy Days

For the next few weeks, the animals worked very hard, cutting the hay and bringing it all in for the winter. Sometimes it was difficult because all the things on the farm, like the machines, were made for humans. But the pigs were clever and found good ways for everyone to do their jobs. The pigs did not actually work, but they told the others what to do and watched over them. Because they understood so much, it was natural for the pigs to be the leaders. They often followed Boxer and Clover in the fields as they pulled the cutting machine, calling, 'Forwards, comrades! Backwards!' In the end, the animals cut more hay than Jones and his men ever had.

All summer, the farm work went wonderfully well. The animals were happier than ever; they had not known that it was possible to be so happy. The food tasted better because it was truly their own food, which they had grown for themselves. And now, with no humans taking most of it, there was more for everyone to eat.

The animals got more rest, too, but everyone worked their hardest, and nobody stole anything or argued or made trouble. Boxer had always done a lot of work, but now he was more like three horses than one. No one could believe how much he did. He asked the cockerel to wake him with an early call each day, and then he got up before the others and pushed and pulled from morning to night, doing all the heaviest work. His answer to every problem was, 'I will work harder!' and he repeated this often.

Nobody on the farm was lazy – well, almost nobody. Mollie did not like getting up in the morning, and sometimes she left work early because she had a stone in her horseshoe. The cat was strange, too. She disappeared when there were jobs to do and only returned at mealtimes. The animals noticed this and asked the cat, 'Where have you been?' But she always gave an excellent answer and smiled warmly at everyone, so it was impossible not to believe her. Old Benjamin the donkey still worked in the same old way. He did what he had to do and no more. If anyone asked him, 'Are you happier now, without Mr Jones here?' he said only, 'Donkeys live a long time.'

On Sundays, there was no work. Breakfast was an hour later than usual, and afterwards, the animals joined together for a special ceremony in the farmhouse garden, where they flew a green flag for Animal Farm from the top of a tall stick. The animals then went into the big barn for the special Sunday meeting. There, they planned the next week's work and discussed new ideas for the farm. It was always the pigs who had these ideas. The other animals voted for their favourite ones, but they could never think of their own. Snowball and Napoleon did most of the talking, but strangely they never agreed about anything. If one of the two had an idea, the other always spoke against it. These meetings always ended with the animals singing *Animals of the world*, and the afternoon was for resting and having fun.

The pigs kept a large room for themselves in one of the farm buildings where they could do their planning and studying. They used books that they had taken from the farmhouse to find out how to fix things on the farm and to get other important information. Snowball started lots of groups to help the animals learn new things, too, like a More Eggs Group for the chickens and a Clean Tails one for the sheep. Most of these groups did not go well, but the reading and writing classes were a great success.

The reading and writing classes were a great success.

By the autumn, almost every animal on the farm could read, some more than others. The pigs could read and write very well. Muriel the goat learned, too, and sometimes read to the other animals in the evenings. Benjamin read as well as the pigs, but never wanted to read anything, and although Clover could not put words together, she learned to read the letters from A to Z. Boxer learned A, B, C, and finally D, and he wrote them every day to stop himself forgetting them. Mollie learned only the five letters in her name. She wrote them on the ground using small sticks and laid flowers beside them to make them pretty.

The other animals learned no more than the letter A, so they could not learn the Seven Commandments. Snowball thought about this, and then said that a single Commandment containing all the ideas of Animalism was enough. The new Commandment, FOUR LEGS GOOD, TWO LEGS BAD, was written on the barn wall above the Seven Commandments, and in bigger letters. All the animals learned it, and the sheep enjoyed lying in the field together and repeating, 'Four legs good, two legs bad. Four legs good, two legs bad' for hours.

Napoleon was not interested in Snowball's groups. He said that teaching the young animals was more important than helping the older ones with their reading. Two of the farm dogs had recently had puppies, and Napoleon said he could teach them everything that they needed to know. He took these nine little dogs away from their mothers to a small room above the pigs' room, and everyone quickly forgot about them.

The animals soon understood where the cows' milk had gone on the day after the Rebellion. The pigs had added it to their own food, and they now did this every day. When the apples were ready to eat, the animals were surprised to hear that there was a new order: all apples were for the pigs only. Even Snowball and Napoleon agreed about this order, and Squealer was sent to explain it to the others.

'Comrades!' Squealer cried, 'Do not think that we're taking the milk and apples because we like them. No, many of us pigs don't like them at all. We're taking them for our health. We work with our heads, and our ideas are very important to the farm and to you all. If we don't take care of you and the farm, Jones will come back. Yes, Jones will come back!' Squealer was now jumping from side to side with his tail moving fast. 'None of you wants to see Jones come back, do you?' he cried.

When it was explained like this, the animals understood. They were sure that they did not want Jones back, and the pigs' health was indeed important, so it was agreed: the milk and apples were only for the pigs.

CHAPTER 5

The First Battle

By late summer, news of what had happened on Animal Farm had travelled across half the country. Every day, Napoleon and Snowball sent birds out to fly to neighbours' farms, where they told the animals about the Rebellion and taught them the song *Animals of the world*.

Jones had spent most of the summer drinking in the pub in Willingdon, telling people about the terrible things that the animals had done to him at Manor Farm (he did not call it Animal Farm). At first, the other farmers laughed about it and said the idea of animals managing a farm was crazy. But when it became clear that Animal Farm was doing well, they were angry and frightened. They did not want rebellions on their own farms, and if they heard their animals singing *Animals of the world*, they beat them.

One day early in October, some of the farm birds flew home with worrying news. Jones and his workers and people from nearby farms were all marching towards Animal Farm, carrying sticks, whips, and guns. Clearly, they wanted to try and take the farm back.

The pigs had planned for this, so Snowball quickly gave his orders, and two minutes later, every animal was where it needed to be. When the humans reached the farm buildings, Snowball began the first part of his battle plan. Thirty-five birds flew over and let their droppings fall on the men's heads, while the bigger birds suddenly appeared on the ground and bit the men's feet and legs. Next, Snowball, Benjamin, Muriel, and all the sheep ran forwards, hitting them hard with their heads. But the men hit the animals back with their sticks and heavy boots, and Snowball told all the animals to run towards the farmhouse.

The humans saw their enemies running away and thought they had won the battle. They began chasing the animals, but in fact, that was what Snowball had planned. When the humans were between the farmhouse and the barns, three horses, three cows, and the rest of the pigs made a circle around them, and Snowball ran as fast as he could towards Jones. Jones saw Snowball coming and shot his gun. The bullets killed a sheep and hit Snowball's back, but Snowball

did not stop running. He threw himself at Jones's legs, and Jones went flying through the air and landed in some sheep droppings.

But the most frightening animal was Boxer, who followed Snowball into the circle. He stood up on his back legs and kicked his large, heavy front feet in the air, hitting the head of a farm boy, who fell to the ground. When the men saw this, some of them dropped their sticks and tried to run, but the animals chased them, hitting, kicking, and biting. Every animal on the farm wanted to fight. Even the cat suddenly jumped off a roof onto someone's back. As soon as they could, the humans ran towards the road, and the birds flew after them, chasing them off the farm.

Every animal on the farm wanted to fight.

Only the farm boy was left on the ground. With one foot, Boxer tried very gently to turn him over. 'He's dead,' he said sadly. 'I didn't want to kill anyone.'

'Comrade,' cried Snowball, 'these things happen in battles. The only good human is a dead one.'

'Where's Mollie?' somebody asked.

Mollie was missing, and for a moment, everyone was worried. But the animals found her hiding in the barn, where she had been since the start of the battle. When they came back out, the farm boy was not there any more. He had in fact not died, and had run away while the animals were looking for Mollie.

The animals all met outside the big barn and talked excitedly about the battle, and then the flag was put up and *Animals of the world* was sung several times. They buried the sheep that had died and decided to make a medal called the Brave Animal Medal. They gave one to the dead sheep and one to both Snowball and Boxer.

The animals discussed a name for the battle, too, and finally agreed on 'the Battle of the Barn' because the battle had started near the barn. Mr Jones's gun was put next to the flag, and they decided to shoot it twice a year: first at a ceremony on the 12th of October to remember the Battle of the Barn, and then at another ceremony on the 21st of June to remember the Rebellion.

CHAPTER 6

Snowball Leaves

When winter arrived, Mollie became more and more difficult. Every morning, she was late for work. She said it was because she did not feel well, but she was never too ill to stop eating. Some of the animals said she was getting sugar and ribbons from a nearby farm. Clover spoke to Mollie about this: 'I thought I saw you looking over the wall to the next farm. The farmer was touching your nose and giving you ribbons or something.'

'No, that's not true!' cried Mollie, moving her feet about on the ground.

But three days later, Mollie disappeared, and later she was seen by some birds with her new owner outside a pub. She was wearing ribbons, and the birds said she looked happy. None of the animals ever talked about Mollie again.

In January, the weather became really cold. The ground was hard and icy, and the animals could do nothing in the fields, but there were a lot of meetings in the big barn. The pigs decided everything at these meetings, although all the animals voted before anything new was started. The only problem was that Snowball and Napoleon did not agree about anything. If one of them had an idea, the other always hated it.

At meetings, most animals agreed with Snowball because his speeches were so good. But between meetings, Napoleon often went and spoke to the animals to try and get them on his side. He was very successful with the sheep, who had started to call, 'Four legs good, two legs bad' a lot, even during meetings. They did this more than ever when Snowball was speaking.

The sheep had started to call 'Four legs good, two legs bad' a lot.

Snowball had lots of clever ideas for the farm. 'We must build a windmill,' he said one day. 'A windmill will make electricity for the farm, and then we'll be able to have lights in the barns at night and use machines to do our work. They'll cut the hay and milk the cows for us, and we'll have more time for rest and to read and learn.'

Snowball read all about how to build a windmill and carefully drew his plans for it on the floor of the little shed that he now used as an office. The other animals came to see the plans every day and thought they looked wonderful, although they were impossible to understand. Even the chickens came to stare at them.

Only Napoleon stayed away. He had been against the idea of a windmill from the beginning. But one day, he arrived at Snowball's office. He walked around heavily, looking closely at the plans and smelling everything. Then suddenly, he lifted his back leg, urinated over the plans, and walked out in silence.

After this, the animals on the farm argued endlessly about the windmill. Snowball said that with a windmill they only had to work three days a week. But Napoleon warned, 'Everyone will become hungry because we won't be able to grow enough food while we're building it.' So there was one group which said, 'Vote for Snowball and a three-day week,' and another group which said, 'Vote for Napoleon and a full food store.'

At last, Snowball's windmill plans were ready for a vote at the Sunday meeting. Snowball stood up and talked excitedly to everyone about the many wonderful reasons for building the windmill. Then, Napoleon stood up to reply. He said quietly that the idea of a windmill was stupid and told the animals to vote against it, then he sat down again. He had only spoken for thirty seconds and did not seem interested in the discussion.

Snowball jumped up again. He had to shout because the sheep were calling, 'Four legs good, two legs bad.' But because he spoke so excitedly about the windmill and knew so much about it, everyone now thought he should win the vote. Then suddenly, Napoleon stood up again. He looked towards Snowball strangely and made a sound with his mouth that nobody had heard before.

There was a terrible growling noise outside and nine big, frightening dogs ran into the barn, straight towards Snowball. He jumped out of the way, only just escaping their teeth, then ran out of the door with the dogs after him. Too frightened to speak, all the animals pushed out through the door to watch the chase. Snowball ran very fast, but the dogs were close behind him. He fell at one moment, and one of the dogs nearly bit his tail, but Snowball got away again and escaped through a hole in the farm wall.

The animals slowly moved back to their places in the barn, silent and afraid. The dogs returned, too, and jumped around Napoleon. At first, no one could think where these dogs had come from, but then they remembered the puppies that Napoleon had kept above the barn. They had grown large – and frightening – and now they followed Napoleon and did everything that he told them, just like Jones's dogs.

Napoleon stood with his dogs where Old Major had been when he had talked to them before the Rebellion, and he told the animals, 'There will be no more of these Sunday Meetings. They aren't needed and take too much time. I'll lead a special group of pigs; we'll meet and tell you what we've decided. We'll still all meet on Sunday mornings beside the flag and sing *Animals of the world*, then everyone will get their orders for the week. There'll be no more discussions.'

Napoleon told the animals, 'There'll be no more discussions.'

Many of the animals wanted to question this terrible news, but they did not know what to say. Even Boxer knew something was wrong. Four young pigs jumped up and tried to speak, but the dogs made frightening noises, and they sat down at once. Then the sheep called, 'Four legs good, two legs bad' loudly for a quarter of an hour, so no more discussion was possible.

Later, Squealer was sent around to talk to everyone. 'Comrades,' he said, 'I hope you understand that Napoleon is doing this for us all. He knows that all animals are equal, but he thinks that, if you decide things, you may get them wrong and put the farm in danger. For example, you listened to Snowball, and now we know he's no better than a criminal.'

'He fought bravely at the Battle of the Barn,' said somebody.

'It's not enough to be brave,' Squealer answered. 'It's more important to obey and to follow orders. Perhaps Snowball didn't fight as bravely as we thought. We must be careful and do what Napoleon tells us at all times. If we don't, our enemies will return. You don't want Jones back, do you?'

That was very true. The animals did not want Jones back, and if meetings made it possible for him to return, they needed to stop. Boxer had had time to think, and he said, 'If Napoleon says something, it must be right.' And after that, he added 'Napoleon is always right' to his favourite words 'I will work harder'.

Spring was coming. Snowball's office was now locked, and the plans that he had drawn on the floor were forgotten. Each Sunday, the animals came together for a short ceremony and watched the flag going up. Then they went into the barn to get their orders for the week, and everyone sang *Animals of the world*, just once, before the short meeting ended.

Three Sundays after Snowball had gone, the animals were surprised to hear that Napoleon now wanted them to build a windmill. He gave no reasons and did not explain why he had changed his ideas about this, but just said, 'There will be two years of extra work to build it. The work will be hard, and there may be less food.'

Later, Squealer explained to everyone that Napoleon had always wanted a windmill. He had pretended not to because Snowball was dangerous, which showed how clever Napoleon was. 'Clever, comrades! Clever, clever,' Squealer repeated many times. In fact, he added, Snowball had *stolen* the plans from Napoleon. But now, because Snowball had gone, they were ready to start building.

The animals did not understand all of this, but because Squealer was so sure, and because the dogs who were with him growled in a frightening way, they accepted what he said.

Chapter 7

The Windmill

That year, the animals were very busy. But they were happy because every job that they did was for them, not for lazy humans. All spring and summer, they worked sixty hours each week, and in August, Napoleon said that they also needed to work on Sunday afternoons.

Building the windmill was the hardest work that they had ever done and very slow. There was a quarry on the farm where the animals found large stones, and together they pulled them up to the top of the quarry, then dropped them over the edge in order to break them into smaller pieces. Everyone helped – the cows, Benjamin, Muriel, and even some of the pigs a few times – but the work was really only possible because of Boxer, who was stronger than any of them.

Building the windmill was really only possible because of Boxer.

It was Boxer who pulled the stones up to the top of the hill where they were slowly building the windmill. He was extraordinary. Clover told him to be careful and take care of himself, but Boxer did not listen. He asked the cockerel to wake him up even earlier in the mornings, and as he worked, he repeated his favourite words, 'I will work harder' and 'Napoleon is always right'.

By late summer, it was clear that the farm needed things that the animals could not make, like metal horseshoes, dog food, and machines for the windmill. One Sunday, Napoleon said to the animals, 'We need money to buy things, so we'll sell some of this summer's hay and a few other things that we grew. And later, if we need more money, we can sell some of the chickens' eggs.'

The animals were surprised when they heard this. They remembered that one of the ideas of Animalism had been never to buy and sell things with money – or they thought they could remember that. The four young pigs once again tried to ask questions, but the dogs immediately growled at them, and the sheep cried, 'Four legs good, two legs bad... ' Napoleon put up a front leg for them to be quiet and continued, 'I've planned everything. Mr Whymper from Willingdon will take care of money and any business. None of you animals will need to talk to him. I'll do this for you myself. Every Monday morning, he'll visit Animal Farm to meet with me.' Then Napoleon cried 'Long live Animal Farm!' and when everyone had sung *Animals of the world*, he told them to go.

Afterwards, Squealer went around the farm and talked to the animals to stop them worrying. 'You're not remembering clearly,' he said to them. 'We never said that we mustn't use money or sell things. That isn't written anywhere, is it?' And because this was true, the animals told themselves that they were indeed probably remembering wrongly.

So Mr Whymper began visiting Napoleon every Monday to get his orders for the week. At about this time, there was another change too: the pigs started to live in the farmhouse. Again, the animals were surprised because they thought they remembered that, after the Rebellion, everyone had agreed never to live there. Squealer had to explain that the pigs needed a quiet place to work because they had so many important things to decide for the farm. And it was right, he said, for the Leader (he had recently started to call Napoleon 'the Leader') to live in a house.

The animals heard too that the pigs were now sleeping in beds. Boxer just said, 'Napoleon is always right'. But Clover went with Muriel to the barn wall and said, 'Please can you read me the fourth Commandment? Doesn't it say that animals must not sleep in beds?'

Slowly, Muriel read: 'Animals must not sleep in beds *with sheets*.' Clover had not remembered that the Commandment had talked about sheets, but it was clearly written there on the wall.

Squealer walked past with some of the dogs at that moment and explained, 'All animals have a bed. Beds *with sheets* are a human thing. So of course, we threw away the sheets from the farmhouse beds. The farmhouse beds are wonderful for our sleep, which we pigs need in order to think well. We don't want Jones back, do we?'

'Indeed, we don't,' the animals agreed, and no more was said about the pigs' beds. Then a few days later, when they heard that the pigs could begin getting up an hour later than them every day, everyone stayed silent about that, too.

When autumn came, the animals were tired but happy. Napoleon had sold a lot of their hay, so they did not have any more food than when Jones was there. But it was all right because they were so excited about the windmill. They had now built half of it and, while the weather was still dry, Boxer even began to work on it at night.

But November brought very bad weather, and they had to stop work because of the wind and rain. Then one night, there was a big storm, and the farm buildings shook all night. The next morning, the animals saw the most terrible thing: the windmill had fallen down. They all ran to the hill where it had stood, and for a while, as they looked at the stones lying on the ground, no one could speak.

At last, Napoleon said quietly, 'Comrades, do you know who came during the night and destroyed our windmill?' Then he shouted, 'It was our enemy, SNOWBALL! Snowball did this, and if he comes here again, we will kill him! I'll give a medal and twenty kilograms of apples to any animal that catches him!'

The animals were surprised and angry to hear that Snowball had destroyed their windmill, and they began to think of different ways to catch him.

'This morning, comrades,' Napoleon cried, 'we will begin building the windmill again. We'll build all winter, even in terrible weather. We need Snowball to know that he cannot stop us. Long live the windmill and Animal Farm!'

'Long live the windmill and Animal Farm!' cried Napoleon.

CHAPTER 8

A Terrible Winter

A cold, snowy winter followed, and the animals started building the windmill again, even in the icy weather. It was very hard work, and they were always cold and hungry. Only Boxer and Clover did not lose hope. Squealer often came out and told the animals that hard work was very good for them. But in fact, what made them continue was Boxer. They saw how he never stopped and heard him say 'I will work harder!' again and again – and they tried to be like him.

By January, there was not enough food on the farm. The animals had not been able to plant very much that year because they were too busy with the windmill. Also, they had not stored their potatoes well, so they were now soft and black from the ice, and the animals could not eat them. It was clear that they must buy food from somewhere.

It was important that no one outside the farm knew about this. Jones had gone to live in another part of the country now, but Napoleon wanted the people who lived nearby to think that Animal Farm was successful. He decided to use Mr Whymper to give this idea to the other farmers in the village. Now, when Whymper came to the farm, the sheep walked past him, talking loudly about eating lots of extra food. Whymper was also taken to the food store, where he saw boxes and boxes full of food. He did not know that they were full of stones, with only a little food on the top.

Napoleon was spending most of his time in the farmhouse, with his big dogs at the door. When he appeared, he always had six dogs with him, and the dogs growled if anyone came near. He often missed meetings, so other important pigs, usually Squealer, came to give Napoleon's orders to the animals.

One Sunday, Squealer told the animals, 'From now, the farm will sell four hundred eggs every week. Then we can buy food for everyone until spring.' The chickens were very angry about the idea of someone taking away their babies, and during the next few days, there was a small Rebellion. The chickens flew up high under the barn roof and tried to hide their eggs there.

The chickens tried to hide their eggs.

OXFORD | BOOKWORMS

Audio Download
Level 3
Animal Farm

You can activate your code only once.

❶ Go to **www.oup.com/elt/download**

❷ Enter your access code. Follow the instructions on screen.

Need help? Email Customer Support at **eltsupport@oup.com**

OXFORD
UNIVERSITY PRESS

ISBN 978-0-19-426751-9

Napoleon soon stopped this Rebellion. 'Anyone who gives food to the chickens will be punished,' he said, and because the dogs watched all the animals carefully, everyone obeyed his orders. Five days later, the chickens had to come down from the roof because they were so hungry. Nine chickens had died in the Rebellion, but Whymper never heard about this, and every week someone from the village came to the farm to take away four hundred eggs.

One evening in spring, Squealer called the animals together and said, 'Comrades, Snowball has been coming to Animal Farm every night and making trouble. He steals our food and drinks our milk, and now he's planning an attack on us with people from the village. And we've discovered a terrible thing. Do you know, Snowball was working with Jones, even before the Rebellion! This explains many things. We saw how he tried to make us lose the Battle of the Barn, didn't we?'

The animals could not believe it when they heard this. They all remembered – or thought they remembered – how Snowball had fought in the battle, and how he had chased the humans off the farm. Even Boxer, who did not usually ask questions, could not understand it. 'I do not believe that,' he said. 'Snowball was very brave during the battle. And we gave him a medal afterwards.'

Squealer answered, 'We made a mistake, comrade. We've found Snowball's secret papers and it's written in there. He was working with Jones to destroy us, but because of our Leader, Comrade Napoleon, they didn't succeed.' Then

Squealer talked about many things that had happened at the battle, and because he described them so clearly, the animals began to think they remembered them, too. But Boxer was still not sure. 'I don't think that Snowball was against us in the battle. He has done bad things in recent times, but not then.'

Squealer stared at Boxer and said slowly, in a cold, hard voice: 'Our Leader, Comrade Napoleon, is sure – he is very sure – that Snowball was working for Jones. It started a long time before the Rebellion.'

'Ah,' said Boxer, 'if Comrade Napoleon says that, it must be right.'

'Good!' cried Squealer, but the others saw how angrily he looked at Boxer. 'I warn you, comrades,' he said as he left, 'watch everyone carefully. Snowball's spies are among us.'

Four days later, Napoleon ordered everyone to come together outside. He walked out of the farmhouse, wearing medals (he had given two to himself), with his nine growling dogs. The animals sat silently in their places, and something made them feel very afraid.

Napoleon looked around icily, then made that strange sound with his mouth that they had heard before. Immediately, the dogs jumped towards the four young pigs that had sometimes questioned things at meetings, and picked them up in their growling mouths. The dogs pulled the pigs across the ground to Napoleon's feet. The pigs' ears were bleeding, and they were crying in fear and pain. The dogs were crazy with excitement from the taste of blood.

The four young pigs were crying in fear and pain.

Then, suddenly, three dogs jumped towards Boxer. Boxer put out his large foot, catching one dog in the air and holding it down on the ground, and the other two dogs immediately ran away. Boxer, who was ready to kill the dog, looked at Napoleon, but Napoleon told him to lift his foot. Boxer did so, and the dog walked away in terrible pain.

When everyone was calm again, Napoleon ordered the four pigs to confess their crimes. It was true, they said, that they had worked with Snowball to destroy the first windmill. When the pigs had finished speaking, the dogs immediately killed them, and in a terrible voice, Napoleon told the other animals to confess their crimes. Three chickens came forwards and said that they had worked for Snowball as well, so they were killed, too. Then the dogs killed a sheep who said that she had urinated in the animals' water under Snowball's orders. This continued, and other animals confessed and were killed until there were many dead bodies lying by Napoleon's feet, and the air was heavy with the smell of blood.

When it was finished, the animals left quietly, shaking and miserable. In the old days, animals had often died on the farm, but now animals were killing other animals, which seemed much worse. They walked slowly to the hill and lay down together. After a long silence, Boxer said, 'I don't understand it. Perhaps we have made very bad mistakes. I think the answer is that we must work harder,' and he went to do some work.

The others all stayed very close together, with Clover in the middle, not speaking. From the hill, they could see all of Animal Farm, with its beautiful, green fields and fruit trees, and the red roofs of the buildings. It was all theirs, and it had never looked so lovely. But now, they had seen animal blood, and that was not what the Rebellion had promised. The picture of the future that had been in Clover's mind when Old Major had spoken to them was not like this. What had she hoped for? Animals that were equal, and free from whips, with enough food and time for resting; animals working together for each other.

Now, with growling dogs watching them all day, the animals were afraid to say what they thought. These were the things that went through Clover's head, although she did not have the words to say them. Slowly, she began to sing *Animals of the world*, and the others joined her. They sang it three times, slowly, sadly, in a way that they had never sung it before. But as they were finishing, Squealer arrived with two dogs. He had a special order from Comrade Napoleon: 'From now, we cannot sing *Animals of the world*.'

'Why?' Muriel asked.

'It was the song of the Rebellion,' he answered, 'and because Animal Farm is successful, there's no need for it now.' Some of the animals wanted to question this, but the sheep started calling, 'Four legs good, two legs bad' and that ended the discussion.

After a few days, the animals could at last think about what had happened. Some of them remembered the sixth Commandment, and they thought it said: 'No animal must ever kill any other animal.' They did not talk about this near the pigs or the dogs, but among themselves they questioned what had happened.

Clover wanted to check the Commandments on the barn wall, so she went to fetch Muriel, who read: '6 No animal must ever kill any other animal *without a good reason*.' Now they understood: they had forgotten the last few words, and in fact, nobody had broken the Commandment. The dogs had only killed animals who had worked with Snowball, so there had been a good reason.

CHAPTER 9

The Battle of the Windmill

That summer, there were lots of stories about Snowball living on one of the nearby farms. Some of the animals said that he was helping farmers who were planning to attack Animal Farm because they were frightened by its success. After that, the pigs did more to keep Napoleon safe. In the farmhouse, he had his own rooms, and four dogs stood by his bed every night, one at each corner. He had his meals alone, and another pig tasted all his food before he ate it.

All Napoleon's orders now came from Squealer or one of the other important pigs, and Napoleon was not often seen. When he did come out of the farmhouse, he had his dogs, but also a black cockerel that walked in front of him, calling 'cock-a-doodle-doo' before Napoleon said anything.

Napoleon now always had his dogs, but also a black cockerel.

In the autumn, after months and months of hard work, the animals finished the windmill. 'Life on the farm will be much better and easier for all of us now,' they agreed. When they thought about this, they forgot how tired they were and ran around the wonderful new building with cries of happiness. Napoleon himself came out to talk to them, with his cockerel and dogs. He told them what a good job they had done. 'The windmill will be called Napoleon Windmill,' he added.

Just a week after the windmill was finished, the attack came. The animals were eating breakfast when some birds flew in and said that fifteen men had already come through the gate, carrying guns. At first, the animals ran bravely towards the men and tried to chase them away, but the men immediately started shooting, and the animals had to run back and hide in the farm buildings. From there, they could only watch what was happening, and even Napoleon did not know what to do. The men stopped at the windmill and took out some big sticks. 'They're going to destroy the windmill!' the animals cried.

'That's not possible,' said Napoleon. 'The walls are too thick. Be brave, comrades.'

But Benjamin was watching the men closely. Two of them were making a hole in the bottom of the windmill. 'Don't you see what they are doing?' he said. 'They're going to put explosives into that hole.'

The animals waited, frightened. A few minutes later, they saw the men running away from the windmill, and then there was the most terrible noise. Everyone except

Napoleon threw themselves to the ground. When they got up again, they saw a large cloud of black smoke where the windmill had once stood. The fear that the animals had felt a moment earlier now disappeared, and they were driven forwards by this terrible thing that the men had done. With an angry cry, they ran out together and attacked their enemies.

It was a wild, violent battle. The men shot again and again, and when the animals were closer, the men hit the animals with their sticks and their boots. A cow, three sheep, and some birds were killed, and most of the other animals were hurt. Even Napoleon, who was giving orders from the back of the group, was shot in the tail. But the men were hurt, too. Boxer had kicked three of them in the head, and a cow had cut open another man's stomach. When Napoleon's dogs suddenly appeared, the men knew that they were in great danger and started to run away. The animals chased them all the way to the bottom of the field, kicking and biting as the men pushed their way through the trees.

The animals had won, but they were tired and bleeding. They walked slowly back to the farm, looking sadly at their dead comrades who lay on the grass, and they stopped for a while at the place where the windmill had stood. Squealer, who strangely had not been there during the fighting, came towards the animals, smiling, 'We have won!'

'What have we won?' asked Boxer. There were bullets in his back leg, and he had hurt his foot.

'Comrades, we have fought back against our enemies and chased them from Animal Farm!' Squealer answered.

'We have won!' said Squealer, smiling.

'But they have destroyed our windmill, after two years of work!'

'That doesn't matter. We can build it again, comrades,' said Squealer. 'Our enemies tried to take our farm from us, and thanks to our great leader, Napoleon, we are still here.'

'Then we have only won what we already had,' said Boxer. His leg was painful, and he was thinking about all the work that he must do in order to build the windmill again. He was eleven now – not a young horse – and, perhaps, he was not as strong as he had been. Boxer had never thought about that before.

But when the animals returned to the farm, they saw the flag flying and heard Napoleon's speech about how well they had fought, and began to think that perhaps they had indeed won something very important. For two days after this, there were songs and ceremonies where they remembered the battle, which Napoleon named The Battle of the Windmill. They buried their dead comrades, and each animal was given an apple. There was a new medal, too, which Napoleon gave to himself.

A few days later, the pigs found twelve bottles of whisky in the farmhouse. That night, the animals heard loud singing there, and someone saw Napoleon running through the garden, wearing Jones's hat.

Another strange thing happened at about this time. One night, the animals heard a noise outside the barn, and when they ran outside, they found Squealer lying on the ground by the wall where the Seven Commandments were written. Next to him was a chair on its side and a pot of white paint. Squealer got up and quickly disappeared into the farmhouse, holding a brush. None of the animals knew what this meant except Benjamin, who understood, but said nothing.

A few days later, when Muriel was reading the Commandments, she saw another one that the animals had remembered wrongly. The fifth Commandment said, 'Animals must not drink *too much* beer or whisky.' She and the others had not remembered the words 'too much'.

Chapter 10

Boxer

Boxer's foot did not get better quickly. The animals had immediately begun building the windmill again, and Boxer worked every day of the week. He did not want the others to know that he was in pain, but in the evenings, he did tell Clover that his foot was worrying him. She made medicine for him with plants, and both she and Benjamin gently told him to stop working so hard. But Boxer did not listen. He wanted one thing only: to see the windmill nearly finished before he retired. In the first days after the Rebellion, the animals had had discussions about when each animal should retire from work. They had agreed that horses should retire when they were twelve – and Boxer's twelfth birthday was only one year away.

The winter was cold again, and there was more work and even less food than before. Squealer brought lots of figures to meetings and told the animals that they had more hay and vegetables than in Jones's time, and that they worked shorter hours and lived longer. And the animals believed every word. They knew that they were often hungry and cold, and that they were usually working when they were not asleep. But they were sure that it had probably been worse before. Interestingly, the pigs seemed to eat enough. In fact, they were getting fatter. A school for young pigs was planned, and on Sundays, pigs began wearing green ribbons on their tails.

At last, Boxer's foot got better, and he worked even harder, but his coat did not shine any more. The others said, 'The spring grass, when it grows, will be good for him.' But the spring grass came, and Boxer did not get stronger. Again, Benjamin and Clover told him to rest, but Boxer did not stop working. Sometimes, when he was pulling heavy stones in the quarry, he tried to say, 'I will work harder,' but the words did not come.

Then one evening, Boxer was working when he fell and could not get up. The animals hurried to him and found him lying on the ground, unable to move. His eyes were closed, and blood was coming from his mouth.

The animals found Boxer lying on the ground.

'Boxer!' Clover cried. 'Are you all right?'

'It doesn't matter. I think that you can finish the windmill without me now. There are plenty of big stones by the new walls that you can use,' Boxer whispered. 'I'll be twelve in a month's time, and now I'm looking forward to retiring. And perhaps, because Benjamin is getting old too, they'll let him retire at the same time.'

'We must get help at once,' Clover said. 'Run, somebody, and tell Squealer what's happened.'

All the animals ran to the farmhouse, while Clover and Benjamin stayed with Boxer. Fifteen minutes later, Squealer arrived. 'I'm very sorry, and Comrade Napoleon is, too,' he said. 'It's unwelcome news when one of the hardest-working animals on the farm becomes unwell. Comrade Napoleon is going to send Boxer to Willingdon Hospital.'

This worried everyone. No animal except Mollie and Snowball had ever left the farm, but Squealer told them that they could not take care of Boxer themselves, and that he had to go to a hospital where they could make him comfortable. Boxer was helped to stand up and walk back slowly to his sleeping place near the barn.

For two days, he rested, and after work, Clover lay beside him and talked with him, while Benjamin kept the flies away from Boxer with his tail. 'If I get better, I will perhaps live for another three years,' Boxer said. 'I'm looking forward to some peaceful days in the fields. I can learn the twenty-two letters that I don't know yet.'

Benjamin and Clover could only be with Boxer after working hours, and it was in the middle of the day when a man came to take Boxer away. The animals were all at work when Benjamin came running to the field. They were surprised because they had never seen Benjamin run before.

'Quick!' Benjamin shouted. 'Come with me! They're taking Boxer away.'

The animals did not wait for orders from the pig who was watching over them. They stopped work at once and ran towards the farm buildings, where they saw a horsebox for carrying animals. Its door was already shut, with Boxer inside.

'Goodbye, Boxer, goodbye,' the animals called. 'We'll see you soon!'

'Don't be stupid,' shouted Benjamin. 'Do you see what's written on the horsebox? "Alfred Simmonds, Seller of the best dog food". Don't you understand? They're going to kill Boxer and make him into dog food.'

There was a terrible sound from the animals, but at this moment, the horsebox began to move slowly away. All the animals ran after it, shouting and crying loudly.

'Get out, Boxer!' Clover called. 'They're taking you to your death!'

For one moment, through the small window at the back of the box, they saw Boxer's nose with its white line down the middle. Then they heard him kicking inside the horsebox. Boxer was trying to get out, but he was not strong enough any more. His kicking became quieter and quieter as the horsebox drove through the gate. Boxer was never seen again.

'Get out, Boxer!' Clover called. 'They're taking you to your death!'

Three days later, Squealer came to tell the animals that Boxer had died in the hospital. He told them that he had been with Boxer just before he died. '"Napoleon is always right," were Boxer's last words,' Squealer said, crying a little. Then he looked around carefully at the animals and said that he had heard some stupid stories that the pigs had sold Boxer as dog food. He explained that the hospital had recently bought the horsebox from a dog food seller and had not yet painted over the name. He said that Boxer had got the best care, which Comrade Napoleon had paid for himself.

The pigs planned a special evening to remember Boxer, and a few nights later, the animals heard loud singing from the farmhouse. The pigs did not get up until lunchtime the next day, and the animals later heard that the pigs had got some money from somewhere to buy whisky for their party.

CHAPTER 11

Visitors at Animal Farm

Years passed. A time came when the only animals still alive who remembered the days before the Rebellion were Clover, Benjamin, and some of the pigs. Benjamin said that being hungry, tired, and not very happy was how life had always been. But the animals were pleased that they were the only animals in England who owned and managed a farm. If they were hungry and worked hard, they did not do it for humans, but for themselves. This filled their hearts with happiness, and they believed the words, 'All animals are equal.'

Clover was old now and had lots of aches and pains. She was fourteen; she had never retired, and in fact, nobody at Animal Farm ever had. They all worked until they died. Napoleon had become a really large, heavy pig, and Squealer could not see well because his face was so fat. Only Benjamin had not changed much, although there was a little more grey around his face, and since Boxer's death, he had become even quieter than before.

The farm was richer now, and larger, too, because the pigs had bought land from nearby farms. But only the pigs and the dogs were richer. The pigs did not work on the land: they were busy with work that the other animals were not clever enough to understand, like looking through notebooks filled with figures. They counted and checked things, had meetings, and planned the other animals' work. 'We are very busy,' Squealer said. But the pigs made nothing and they did not grow any food, although they ate a lot.

The windmill was finished, but it did not make electricity, and the animals did not get the lights that they had hoped for or their three-day week. Napoleon said that those things were against Animalism, and that the truest happiness came from working hard and living quietly.

One evening, when the animals had finished work for the day, they heard a terrible cry from Clover near the farmhouse. They ran to join her, and saw what she had seen. It was a pig walking on his back legs.

It was a pig walking on his back legs.

Yes, it was Squealer. He was walking across the farmhouse garden on two legs and doing it well enough. A moment later, a line of pigs came out of the farmhouse, all walking on their back legs. Finally, Napoleon appeared, with the black cockerel in front, and dogs growling around him. He, too, was walking on his back legs, and he carried a whip.

There was a deadly silence. For a moment, the animals were too surprised to say anything. But before any of them were brave enough to speak out against something which was so terrible and so wrong, the sheep began calling – loudly – a new song which Squealer had taught them that week. 'Four legs good, two legs *better*. Four legs good, two legs *better*,' they repeated again and again.

By the time the sheep were quiet, the pigs had marched back indoors. Clover gently touched Benjamin's side and walked with him to the end of the barn where the Commandments were written.

'I can't see well now,' she said, 'but that wall looks different. Are the Seven Commandments still the same?'

There was nothing there now except one Commandment. Benjamin read: ALL ANIMALS ARE EQUAL, BUT SOME ANIMALS ARE MORE EQUAL THAN OTHERS.

After that, it did not seem strange that the pigs carried whips when they watched the others working. It did not seem strange that in the farmhouse, the pigs read newspapers and magazines, talked on a new telephone, and put on Jones's clothes. Napoleon himself appeared wearing a black coat and trousers, and his favourite girlfriend wore Mrs Jones's best dresses.

A week after this, some people drove up the road to the farm. The pigs had asked some farmers from the nearby villages to come and look at the farm. They showed them everything, and the visitors liked what they saw.

That evening, the animals heard loud laughing and singing from the farmhouse. Quietly, they walked up to the windows and carefully looked in. Six farmers and six of the most important pigs were sitting around the long table, drinking together. Napoleon was sitting at one end of the table, and they were all playing a game of cards.

As the animals watched, one of the farmers stood up to say a few words. 'In the past,' he said, 'some of us farmers were worried by the idea of a farm that was managed by animals. But Animal Farm is an example to farmers everywhere. I think I'm right when I say that the less important animals on Animal Farm do more work and get less food than the animals in any of our farms. Indeed, we have seen many ideas here that we want to use ourselves. And we all wish Animal Farm success.'

Then Napoleon got up to speak. 'I'm very pleased that we now understand each other,' he said. 'For a long time, some people were saying that we wanted rebellions on other farms. That was not true. We've always wanted to live peacefully with our neighbours and do business with them.

'We've made some changes recently, which I think you'll also be pleased about,' he went on. 'In the past, we had a strange way of calling each other "comrade." But we're stopping this. There will be no more marching or singing on Sundays. And there is one more thing. In your speech, you wished success to Animal Farm. But we're not going to use that name any more. From today, the farm is called Manor Farm again.'

'*I'm pleased that we now understand each other,*' said Napoleon.

When they heard this, the farmers laughed and smiled, and the drinking continued. But as the animals outside watched, they noticed something strange: something that had changed in the faces of the pigs.

The farmers and the pigs had begun playing cards again, but in minutes they were arguing about the game. Twelve voices were shouting angrily, and they were all alike. And now the animals outside the window understood what had happened to the faces of the pigs. They looked from pig to man, and from man to pig, and from pig to man again – and they could not say who was who.

attack *(v & n)* to start fighting or hurting somebody or something; when a person or animal fights someone or something

barn *(n)* a large building on a farm; a farmer keeps animals in it, or food for animals

beer *(n)* an alcoholic drink; if you drink too much beer, you can feel sick

believe *(v)* to be sure that something is true

bury *(v)* to put something (e.g. a dead body) in the ground

ceremony *(n)* an important time when people come to a place or building to do special things, like singing and giving speeches

cock-a-doodle-doo *(n)* a loud sound that a cockerel makes

commandment *(n)* an important idea or rule about how you should live your life

comrade *(n)* a person who believes the same things as the person who is speaking, or someone who belongs to the same group

confess *(v)* to tell someone about something that you have done which was wrong

discussion *(n)* a conversation about somebody or something

droppings *(n)* the poo of some animals, like birds and sheep

electricity *(n)* electricity is used for things like lights, heating buildings, and driving machines

equal *(adj)* the same

explosive *(n)* When you put an explosive in something, it explodes, and the thing breaks into lots of little pieces.

gate *(n)* a kind of door outside, usually in a wall around the edge of a garden, park, or farm

growl *(v)* the frightening sound that an animal makes when it is angry; **growling** *(adj)*

hay *(n)* dry grass that farmers give to their animals to eat

human *(n & adj)* a person; not an animal

kick *(v)* to hit with your foot

lead *(v)* to be the most important person in a group and tell others what to do; **leader** *(n)* the person who leads

long live *(phr)* something that people say when they want somebody or something to live for a long time

medal *(n)* A medal is usually round and made of metal. You may get one when you do something very well (e.g. win a race).

meeting *(n)* a time when people meet to discuss something

milk *(v)* to take milk from an animal, like a cow or goat

paint *(v & n)* you put paint on things, like paper or walls, to give them a colour; **paintbrush** *(n)* a brush that people use to paint with; **painted** *(adj)* when something is covered in paint

quarry *(n)* a place where large stones are taken from the ground

rebellion *(n)* when people attack their leader and try to make them leave because they want a new leader

remind *(v)* to help somebody remember something

retire *(v)* to leave your job and stop working because you are old

ribbon *(n)* a pretty piece of material that you can wear in your hair

shed *(n)* a small building like an outside cupboard

speech *(n)* a talk that a person gives to a group of people

store *(v & n)* to keep something safely; a place where you keep something safely

urinate *(v)* to pee; when water leaves your body

vote *(v & n)* When there is a vote, every person can decide between different things or people. The thing that gets the most votes is the winner.

whip *(n)* a long piece of leather for hitting people or animals

whisky *(n)* an alcoholic drink that is stronger than beer

windmill *(n)* a tall, often round building with parts that turn. Windmills can change the power of the wind into electricity.

cockerel *(n)*

donkey *(n)*

goat *(n)*

horse *(n)*

pig *(n)*

puppy *(n)*

The Russian Revolution

George Orwell wrote *Animal Farm* in the 1940s, during the Second World War, when Joseph Stalin was the leader of Russia – or the Soviet Union, as the country was then called. Orwell wanted to write about how badly Stalin was leading his people and how hard life was there. How had Stalin become the kind of leader that he was – a terrible, frightening dictator?

Joseph Stalin

In 1917, many years before Orwell wrote *Animal Farm*, there had been a revolution in Russia – like the Rebellion at Manor Farm, but the Revolution was a really big change in all of the country. Before the Revolution, many working people and soldiers were very poor, and their lives were hard. They had new ideas about how to make life fairer, and they had had enough of the Tsar – a king who led the country with other rich people. At last, the Tsar was chased from his palaces and the Revolution was successful. Russia was now called the Soviet Union.

Vladimir Lenin had been one of the Revolution's leaders and became the Soviet Union's first leader. But life continued to be hard for people under Lenin. The war had made the country poorer, and some of the ideas of the Revolution were soon forgotten. People had to follow Lenin's orders, and those who Lenin thought were enemies were punished, put in prison, or killed.

After Lenin died, Stalin became leader with two other men, but he fought against them (like Napoleon does against Snowball), and life soon became even worse in the Soviet Union. People were not free and were frightened to say what they believed. People who did not follow orders were made to work very hard in terrible factories and other awful places. Millions died.

Orwell wanted to warn the world about the dangers of leaders like Lenin and Stalin, who become dictators. He probably chose to write a fable – a short, simple story about animals – to hide that he was talking about Stalin's Soviet Union. But he was also thinking about other revolutions, and many other dictators, like Adolf Hitler. Orwell warned that a Revolution can start with ideas about fairness, but things can go wrong when leaders forget that everyone is equal.

READ & RESEARCH Read 'Beyond the Story' and find the answers to these questions.

1 When was the Russian Revolution? Why did it happen?

2 Why did Orwell probably write a fable to talk about Lenin and Stalin?

3 Find another famous fable. What happens in the story? What is the story's message?

dictator *(n)* a leader who gives orders to people and does not let anyone say or think anything different to them

revolution *(n)* a big rebellion in a country when people chase away a king, queen, or leader and bring in new ideas

war *(n)* fighting between countries or between groups of people

Think Ahead

1 **Read about the story on the back cover. Answer the questions.**

1 Why do the animals of Manor Farm chase Mr Jones away?

2 Did the animals get plenty of food and rest when Mr Jones was there?

3 Why do the pigs become the leaders of the farm?

4 Do things go well once the pigs are the new leaders?

2 **What do you think is going to happen in the story?**

1 What starts to go badly wrong after the pigs become the leaders of the farm?

a The animals start to miss Mr Jones.

b The animals do not have enough food.

c The horses want to become leaders, too.

2 What kind of leaders are the pigs?

a They take good care of the animals on the farm, and they help with all the farm work.

b They make the animals work hard, without enough rest.

c They manage the farm cleverly and have many good ideas, which they always discuss with the other animals before they change anything.

3 What happens at the end of the story?

a Mr Jones comes back to Manor Farm.

b The animals chase the pigs away.

c The pigs become like people.

Chapter Check

CHAPTER 1 Complete the sentences with names in the story.

Benjamin   Boxer   Mr Jones   Old Major

1 The farmer, _____, went up to bed.

2 _____ had a strange dream.

3 _____ was as strong as two horses.

4 _____ was the oldest animal, and he was often cross.

CHAPTER 2 Choose the correct words to complete the sentences.

1 The animals wanted to be ready for the *Rebellion* / *spring*.

2 Snowball and Napoleon did all the *planning* / *moving*.

3 Squealer was good at *having* / *explaining* new ideas.

4 Animalism was a new way of *thinking* / *singing*.

5 The Rebellion happened one day when the animals were not given their *milk* / *food*.

CHAPTER 3 Put the events in order.

a The animals stared at the nice things in the farmhouse.

b Snowball wrote 'ANIMAL FARM' on the gate.

c The animals destroyed the humans' whips.

d The animals went to cut the hay, and the milk disappeared.

e The animals all agreed with the Seven Commandments.

CHAPTER 4 Match the sentence halves.

1 The pigs did not actually work because...

2 Boxer's answer to every problem was...

3 At Sunday meetings, Snowball and Napoleon did most of the talking, but...

4 Napoleon said he could teach the nine little puppies...

5 'If we pigs don't take care of you and the farm...

a everything that they needed to know.

b it was natural for them to be the leaders.

c 'I will work harder!'

d Jones will come back,' cried Squealer.

e strangely they never agreed about anything.

CHAPTER 5 Correct the <u>underlined</u> words.

1 The other farmers said the idea of animals managing a farm was <u>wonderful</u>.

2 The humans were marching angrily towards Animal Farm, carrying sticks, <u>flowers</u>, and guns.

3 <u>Napoleon</u> quickly gave his orders, and two minutes later every animal was where it needed to be.

4 The most frightening animal was <u>Mollie</u>, who followed Snowball into the circle.

5 The farm boy had not died and had <u>hidden</u> while the animals were looking for Mollie.

CHAPTER 6 Are the sentences true or false?

1 Mollie was seen with her new owner, looking sad.

2 Napoleon urinated over Snowball's plan for the windmill.

3 Napoleon told them there will be no more discussions.

4 Four young goats tried to speak.

5 'Napoleon had never wanted a windmill,' Squealer said.

CHAPTER 7 Match the sentences with the names in the story.

Boxer Mr Whymper Napoleon Squealer the pigs

1 'I will work harder' and 'Napoleon is always right.'

2 They started to live in the farmhouse.

3 'We don't want Jones back, do we?'

4 He visited Animal Farm every Monday to get his orders.

5 'Comrades, we will begin building the windmill again.'

CHAPTER 8 Complete the sentences with the correct words.

afraid angrily angry brave clearly

1 The chickens were _____ and there was a rebellion.

2 Squealer described the battle very _____.

3 'Snowball was _____ during the battle,' said Boxer.

4 Squealer looked at Boxer _____.

5 The animals were _____ to say what they thought.

CHAPTER 9 Put the events in order.

a The second attack on the farm happened a week later.

b The pigs had a party, and Napoleon wore Jones's hat.

c The animals finished the windmill in the autumn.

d Muriel noticed another commandment that the animals had remembered wrongly.

e Benjamin watched men making a hole in the windmill.

f 'We have won,' Squealer said. 'We can build it again.'

CHAPTER 10 Correct the <u>underlined</u> words.

1 Boxer told <u>Squealer</u> that his foot was worrying him.

2 'You can finish the windmill without me. I'm looking forward to retiring,' said <u>Benjamin</u>.

3 The animals were often hungry and cold, but interestingly the pigs were getting <u>nicer</u>.

4 Boxer was not sent to hospital, but to his <u>bed</u>.

5 Squealer said that stories that the pigs had sold Boxer as <u>a working horse</u> were stupid.

CHAPTER 11 Are the sentences true or false?

1 'Being hungry, tired, and not very happy was how life had always been,' Benjamin said.

2 All the animals at Animal Farm retired at eleven.

3 The windmill made electricity for all the animals.

4 Clover saw a pig, Squealer, walking on his back legs.

5 Napoleon changed the farm's name back to Manor Farm.

Focus on Vocabulary

1 Complete the sentences with the correct words.

believe   equal   leader   remind   vote

1 At first, the animals helped to decide on changes to the farm because they could _____ at meetings.

2 After Snowball was chased away from Animal Farm, Napoleon became the only _____.

3 Squealer liked to _____ the animals that they did not want Jones back.

4 An important commandment that the pigs forgot was that all animals are _____.

5 Boxer did not _____ that Snowball had tried to make the animals lose the Battle of the Barn.

2 Replace the <u>underlined</u> words with the words below.

growled   humans   kicked   stored   whips   windmill

1 Jones and his farm workers always hit the animals with <u>long pieces of leather</u>.

2 At the end of the Battle of the Barn, the animals chased all the <u>people</u> off the farm.

3 Snowball wanted the animals to build a <u>special building</u> to make electricity for the farm.

4 Boxer <u>hit with his foot</u> hard at the attackers.

5 The dogs <u>made a frightening sound</u>.

6 The potatoes had not been <u>kept</u> well.

Focus on Language

1 **Read the text and <u>underline</u> the past perfect verbs.**

From the hill, they could see all of Animal Farm. It was all theirs, and it had never looked so lovely. But now they had seen animal blood, and that was not what the Rebellion had promised. So what had it promised?

2 **Complete the sentences with past perfect verbs.**

1 What picture of the future _____*had*_____ Clover _____*seen*_____ (see) in her mind when Old Major _____ (speak) to them?

2 What _____ Clover _____ (hope) for?

3 Clover _____ (not forget) the words of Old Major's song.

3 **Read this text from the story and <u>underline</u> the personal pronouns.**

Squealer talked about many things that had happened at the battle, and because he described them so clearly, the animals began to think they remembered them, too.

But Boxer was still not sure. 'I don't think that Snowball was against us in the battle. He has done bad things in recent times, but not then.'

4 DECODE **Who or what does each pronoun stand for in exercise 2? Use the words below.**

Boxer   Snowball   Squealer   the animals
things that happened in the battle

Discussion

1 Read the sentences giving opinions in the story. Who is speaking?

　1 <u>I'm sure that</u> a time will come when animals stand up against humans.

　2 <u>I strongly believe that</u> Napoleon is always right.

　3 <u>To be honest</u>, pigs need to have the apples and milk because we work with our heads.

　4 <u>In my opinion</u>, we will only have to work a three-day week if we build a windmill.

　5 <u>We agree with</u> Napoleon: FOUR LEGS GOOD, TWO LEGS BETTER!

　6 <u>I think that</u> I'm an excellent leader and Animal Farm is very successful.

2 **THINK CRITICALLY** Do you think the opinions in exercise 1 are right or wrong? Why?

3 Give your opinion about *Animal Farm*. Answer these questions. Use the <u>underlined</u> words in exercise 1.

　1 Is *Animal Farm* a good story? Why / Why not?

　2 Who is your favourite character? Why?

　3 What message is Orwell trying to give us?

4 **COMMUNICATE** Take turns to give your opinions from exercise 3 to a partner. Are they the same or different?

1 Read the online guide at a museum about the French Revolution.

THE FRENCH REVOLUTION

Here you can see a painting of the King of France, Louis the Sixteenth, riding a horse. King Louis and the people around him took too much money from everyone in the country, and they lived well while many people were poor. Nobody could choose what happened or vote for change and, in July 1789, there was a rebellion. People in Paris attacked the Bastille, which was a castle and prison. This was the beginning of years of change, difficulty, and war for the country.

In January 1793, Louis the Sixteenth was killed by the people who were leading the revolution. The leaders of the revolution changed many times, and people believe that some were awful dictators, like a man called Maximilien Robespierre, who you can see in this painting.

There was even a time called the Terror, which was terrible, violent, and frightening. After the Revolution, France has almost never had a king or queen as its leader again. Why do some leaders become dictators after fighting for more fairness and equality?

2 Answer these questions about the French Revolution using the information in the online museum guide.

1 When did the French Revolution start?

2 Who was chased away?

3 Why did the Revolution start?

4 Does anything about the revolution remind you of something that happened in the story *Animal Farm*?

3 Now think about an important time or moment in your country's past, and answer the questions about it.

1 What is the name of this moment in history?

2 When did it start?

3 What happened?

4 Which person or people are very well-known for this moment in the past? Why?

5 Does anything about this moment remind you of the story *Animal Farm*?

4 **CREATE** Use your answers in exercise 3 to write an online museum guide about your chosen moment in the past.

5 **COMMUNICATE** Read a partner's online guide. Can you answer the questions in exercise 3 using your partner's online guide?

If you liked this Bookworm, why not try...

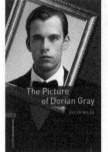

The Picture of Dorian Gray

LEVEL 3
Oscar Wilde

'When we are happy, we are always good,' says Lord Henry, 'but when we are good, we are not always happy.'

Lord Henry's lazy, clever words lead the young Dorian Gray into a world where it is better to be beautiful than to be good; a world where anything can be forgiven – even murder – if it can make people laugh at a dinner party.

The Three Strangers and Other Stories

LEVEL 3
Thomas Hardy

On a stormy winter night, a stranger knocks at the door of a shepherd's cottage. He is cold and hungry, and wants to get out of the rain. He is welcomed inside, but he does not give his name or his business. Who is he, and where has he come from? And he is only the first visitor to call at the cottage that night...

In these three short stories, Thomas Hardy gives us pictures of the lives of shepherds and hangmen, dukes and teachers. But rich or poor, young or old, they all have the same feelings of fear, hope, love, jealousy...
